The Unyielding Paradox

by

Miles Goodwin

DORRANCE PUBLISHING CO
EST. 1920
PITTSBURGH, PENNSYLVANIA 15238

Dorrance Publishing Co
585 Alpha Drive
Pittsburgh, PA 15238
Visit our website at www.dorrancebookstore.com

ISBN: 979-8-89211-032-7
eISBN: 979-8-89211-530-8

The Unyielding Paradox

Feast

I have taken you behind dumpsters and in godless sheets
I have built a garden in you
In courtyards and greenhouses
I have brought out the unholy howls in sunsets
And given pleasure to the moaning knight
Whose sword shall be passed under starry sky
All of this was done with generosity and truth
Why
I will not hold you longer than a day
Yet
I find myself tracing the lines on your dried fruit
And tasting its juice until next we meet
It makes me rebuke the cold premonition
Of flaws and light on such a face
I wait here for you
To damage the weary heart
So
I may find myself in another
I am a hungry man
Wanting more
Such truths are vanity and nothing more
Let me feast once more
And I swear I shall be full for a life
One more taste
Until the vine dries
How can you be
Less hungry than me

Resurrection

Sit beneath my feet
And I will tell you of Rome
The glory and gore
How
We built bones
Upon bones
And
How
I resurrected the city
From the blood
Of the sun

Icarus's Dream

Cities burn
At the spark of your touch
The winter wind howls
Yet it doesn't say much
Your hand
Feels like a priceless artifact
To a wealthy king
How
Did it feel
To fly close to the sun
How
Lonely was it
To dream

A wonderful dream

She believed
A dream of making love
To the gravestones
Who
Burned before her
At
Least
The bones
Gave weight to her heavy life

Purgatory's Delight

I,
The virgin,
Sat bloody at your altar
Not by request
But by choice
I kneel for your honor
And the glory
Between your legs
I present the disgraceful sacrifice
And the relics of my past
Take my song
Take it and run
For
You are the one
Who
Did not birth me
But gave me life
You are the solemn judge
That shall not be overruled
You are heaven
You are hell

The High Court

Late afternoon
We sat
Beneath the sunlit glow
I gave you respect
And you gave me honor
We reaffirmed the impossible belief
And pardoned each other of our brazen crimes
Still we remained married
To our invisible worlds
Your work
My plan
You slept
And the dogs played gleefully
Sitting in the loneliest of courts
Who
Will
Be the judge now

Summer Nights

Lay here
Where
They cannot see
On a bed of dandelions and whisper to me
The willows
They open the sky
And shimmer like sunless stars
The movie is over
Your hand in my pants
Now
We sleep

Youth Expired

He lay beside him
A boy
Who
Dared to be a man
Nothing spoken
Only an untethered dream
From his quivering lips
His company in dark times

White Flags

She started the war
And I started the fire
Now
We sit having tea
Strangers
To the violence

A King's Wish

On the night he made my mouth his throne

I lost my ambitions

The feeling was doom

But my chest

A mere cloud

Rising to the occasion

I want his promise

I want it in blood

And I want it on my lips

I want inside you

Still,

That is a luxury I cannot afford

A beast yet to be tamed

I ask

That this be enough

That my fruited tree

Be enough to bear

Your burden and to feed your flesh

The way you feed mine

May this be your forever

And my death

All in the name of the crown

For

You are what I worship

What

I crave

But may this parting gift be enough

A fond memory

The Unspoken Affair

This is a revolution
A new beginning
Of capital sin
And a meeting of flesh
What
Was used up
Will now be revived
The petals of your delicate flower
Reborn
In the image of moon
Together we will shine
The cracks in the morning glory
Wait
My husband calls
He sinks beneath the contrary belief
That our boat
Has not sailed
But age has returned
And we are stuck beneath
The bridge of Sing
A mark on the unity of truth
A cherry in the birth of intimacy
That cannot be declined
Only to be born
Through gravity and jealousy
Look
See how she walks
The steps of a virgin
On cathedral stairs

THE UNYIELDING PARADOX - 11

And him in her gown
Now
See his mannerisms
Watch him dissolve
Into the stranger's grasp
Another star banned
From the heavens

Morning Glory

The blood
I crave
Cold to the touch
Engorging my fantasies
She comes to me
In my sleep
How
Dare I say more
I deserve less
Than soaked hands
And midnight streets
But winds change
And seasons come
So
Here are my hands
Holding the gun
With feet too afraid to run
Now
Irony must
Bite the dust

Summer's Kiss

It was late summer
When he touched me
Gathering my thorns
And painting my soul
With fingers so agile and soft
He gave me life
In the heatless night
It was late summer
And we lay cheek to cheek
His shirt drenched in sweat
Speaking little
He became the vessel
To which
I lived and found the world
It was late summer
And the flames
He lit burned
Deep into the hottest temptation
His confidence held me close
When
All others chose not to see

Queen of Coins

The queen graces a casket
Her rosebud
A weapon to the masses
Now
Nailed to the church doors
With temptation's love
Buried with the secrets of the men
Who
Do not lay still
I cannot say
Only sit and mummer
And her lost beauty
Beauty in disarray
Beauty be humbled
Rise from your crypt
And your blood-soaked sheets
And radiate the opulent indulgences
From a poor man's anxious desires
Come to me in the night
And be the light
That caresses the notes
Of the musical rebirth
I will serve you
For as long as
Both sides of the coin exist
I am
Your worshipper

Indebted

Years
And I can still hear what he said
Unable to enact it
I bend with the weeping roses
And rise with the roosters
To help out
In the ways I saw fit

Meeting of Worlds

Hand in hand
He took me beneath the snow
Entering me he clenched with relief
My body of loneliness
Torn from within
And seen without
He embraced what I failed to
Now
He exhales at the sight
And whispers ever so plainly
You are love

Moonbeams

The moon hangs high in her disregard
She is uncomplicated
She is regal
I should admire her
I should be grateful to be beneath her allure
But I am a poor lover
Of the moon, I am sure
I take her at face value and nothing more

Beauty Be Brief

Sailboats on silver seas
Traces of salt on your cheek
The world
At your fingertips
Sudden and breathtaking
A moment
The God's speak about

A Lover's Treaty

There is another
A heart
That guides me to the broken
Reject it
I cannot
She bares my face
And speaks my tongue
How
Willing she must be
To come
To my hell with me

An Open Book

Lay back
On your endless spine
Let me lick my fingers
And turn your pages
Together we will reveal
The happiest of endings

On Wings She Sings

There is no
Stronger air
Than
The breath
Of a morning dove

Collective Souls

I met a man
Solemn and blue
He cried about the city
And I thought of you
How
We both lost everything
We thought
We'd always knew

Contracted Lovers

The elderly have wisdom
The young have life
So, will you
Marry me
And we can consecrate this marriage
In an unburdened strife

Love in Lothian

Lover come lay beside me
If you are to be true
Be sweet
Be gentle
Until the day I ask for more
Then let us hang ourselves from each rung
And manifest our future
As the taste escapes our tongue
Until love is scorned
And winter days be forlorn
May every battle be won
And our hopes for freedom
Forever undone
This is the look I give to you
My love

Back to Babylon

I rebelled against normality
And lived between his legs
I punished myself with his kiss
And took another to bed
I caught our words
In the palm of my hand
He sat on my face during the war
And dragged me to Babylon
Where
My lips could not find the strength to speak
The bells overhead echoing
Taunting
And reviling
In the tongue that cannot move
Back to paradise I must go
Before conversation
Alludes me
Once more

King of Silence

Dear King of Silence
I knew you once
And thanked you with my solitude
Now we must go to war
With the bits of soul that remain
To speak once more
And to say nothing less

Haunted House

Our house now exists with ghosts
There is one to bring us tea
One to serve us dinner
One to watch us shower
One to watch us make love
And one to take it back
They hide in the cracks of our mirror
Fly with the doves
But we cannot let them take this dance
No
They cannot have this waltz
They cannot have this waltz

Tower of Babylon

To the river's edge I went
Dark and scathed
I walked to Babylon
Though I did not utter a word
I hummed her name
Spoke her chords
I had no strength
She saw me there
Collapsed at the gates
Her beauty still quite upon my lips
Yet
When I came from the sand and stone
To the grandeur of it all
I only said one word
Now lost
To the tower
Lost to her

Madison Avenue

My coffee is still full
And I sit
At a coffee shop on Madison Avenue
Beguiled by horns
Waiting for you
To come
Home

Streetlights

My dear
I have found a place to call home
I went out for a drink
And saw you standing there
Beneath the stolen light
I bowed before you
To stay in your grace
And the stars rejoiced in this manner
The streetlights lifted me
To a place only you may go
And the horns
Took me home
Back to benevolence
Back to alone
Now
I sit here
Water in hand
Praying for peace
Dying in sand

Take Me There

Hold me
When
The snake's recoil in elegy
And the birds sing their funeral songs
Maybe then
I could stand the sun
And what she claims to give
Until then
I give you this hand
And pray to you
It's not too late
For one last
Date
Steeped in Saturn
And her stars
I drink from her Holy Grail

To The Man I Love

I hear the traffic below
It helps me sleep
But I love my coffee
And I love my sickness
There will come another day
To rise and stall
To fend off a friend
To not make the call
I love him
He is a gentle soul
Still
I am no fool
But he smiles
His eyes are stone
And my heart glass
To say I envy him
Would be a disservice
To a man such as him
To the man
I love

Between the Lines

I awake to panic
The flowers have died
And the birds they sing
I could've changed the water
Cut the stems
I could've found a deeper vase
Or a sunnier place
Would it matter
If I stood them up straight
And let them not lay
Would
They grow in the night
And die by day
I awake to panic
And the cliffs call my name
To echo on their majesty
So
I won't sleep
Or dream of traffic
Or the one who sits beside me
On Saturdays
But would anyone
Really care
About the details

My Queen

My darling
She stood up today
And fell in my arms
She had danced the salsa
With pinot on her lips
She used to dance
To stomp her feet
And to cry
Now she holds her head down
Beneath a bruising crown
She is sick
But does not confess to rage
Something
I cannot avoid

Space, Needle

Taking me back
I relive Seattle
His yellow hair
My clothes blue
With regret
At five
We would grab dinner
And mask our sounds
Beneath the traffic below
I told him not to wait
Not to be sorry for me
But we could only sustain
Pleasure for so long
Until the last time
I drove you home
And drove you mad
Now the space needle
Is still grand
It's still great
I am drunk
Nothing has failed
Only ended
And maybe
That's the way
It should be
A body without you
And space for me

Battlefront

I'll wear this uniform
To fight in our unholy war
Day and night
I'd stand by your side
Taking bullets
And casting lies
To the passage of time
There will be but one winner
On the day this ends
And heroes
Bare their thorns
I will pour a glass of wine
And smell the roses
For once
For once

Our House, My Home

I dream of you
For many nights
A god among men
Who
Entered my doorway
Breaking the seal
It was then that I realized
My house
Is a frail notion

Susanne

I have waited
Longer than I have lived
For a love
More than a season
Nobody mentions spring
But I know her well
Her hair is gone
Her cheeks sunken in
She comes on the morning boat
She leaves by a midnight train
A love in vain
Here she comes now
My dearest Susanne

Through Her for Him

His black hair
An onyx blade in the night
Cutting through me
And my sharpest edges
This is the man
I broke my wife for
This is the man
Who stole my house
Still I come to him
And worship at his feet
As if saints could walk on land
More than a stranger
He is the heat
That shares this bed
Burning me as I live
But I cannot think
Of a more beautiful way
To die

My Soul and Me

I heard my soul sing
Among the bushes and leaves
Plucked from stone
She sang in harmony
With you
Her chords
Heaven
Her notes alluring wilderness
That begged to be explored
Still she stayed
There
Tucked away
From the world to see
That she was mine
And I belong to thee
Forever in harmony
My soul
And me

Morning Meditation

I had breakfast with your ghost
We had coffee and cold toast
We spent the meal
Talking about our living days
I had breakfast with your ghost
We sat outside
In the forgotten sunlight
Warming our translucent humor
I had breakfast with your ghost
When
It was time for you to go
I held the cavernous door
To the depths below
And kissed you
With
The stillness of a rose
I had breakfast with your ghost
You thanked me for my generosity
And we promised to do it again soon
I had breakfast with your ghost
And
Now
I know you

Closeted Works

Put me somewhere
Against a wall
Or in the darkest night
Objectify me
In the ways of a Saint
Worship at my flesh
And drink my body
Find the places
Where
Others have hidden
But you now exist
Speak it into existence
And flood me
With the desires
Of your tongue
So
I may speak
Your closeted truth

Unearth Me

Grab my hair
And bury the graves
Deep in me
Whisper to me
The secrets of your ancestor
So
That I may hear them clear
Hold me
On the verge of life
And keep my soul
In your hands forever

Grandest Regrets

My apologies for the sudden sorrow
And asking you to sleep
With me in the snow
This was not the workings of love
This was scorn
And the taste of a new lover
Beyond my lips
I came to heal
But was never reborn
So, I will dwell in your hallway
Half-sober and asking for forgiveness
This is us
This is marriage
A failed ideology

Serene Grace

I wanted to trace
The lines on her face
With an authentic grace
To know the creases
And the stories they faced
To be one with her
In the most intimate way
Beyond sound and taste
To be intimate
Without losing my place

Morning View

Morning dew
Drifts across
The unassuming face
Curled in silken sheets
Hair cascaded across
The sea of pillows
Asleep
But awakening my heart
This is
What
It means to dream awake

My Stolen Myth

They hang from you lips
The steps
To Babylon
I would climb them
To reach your stars
Now speech fails
The weak
Another myth
Has gone extinct

Interactive Exhibit

Art
Is a delicacy to the
Eyes
And perhaps
That is
Why
I could
Feast on you
All night

My Dance with Evelyn

Dance
With your foot
On mine
And we will sashay away
To another moment
When
Both our feet
Were perfectly
In time
I walk
With the night
Her heart
A ripe apple
That many want to bite
Only to find
Ripe fruits
Decay the fastest

Night Pleasures

My secrets
In her hand
Burying them
In the stars
That adorn her
Darken clothes
She whispers
To me
Her pleasure
Before the day
Seeks
To
Win the
Measure

Dare to Speak

She
Suffocated
In a tongue
That was not
Her own

Songbirds and Snakes

She lives now
In the ballad
Of songbirds
And snakes
Which side
She chose
Lives in
The breath
She did not
Take

Beauty Unencumbered

Water
Or wine
She ages
With a beauty
Not controlled
By
Time

Constellations

I will
Drape
Myself
In the stars
To be close
To your
Sun

Bluebird

Under
The willow
The bluebird sings
Of nights
And the city street
Where she once
Made her nest
And where
She now
Lays her
Children
To rest

Through the Orchard

We walked
Past the lilac trees
Watching the clouds
Swim in the endless sea
All the while
Unaware
That our feet
Stood still
And our patience
Became a game
And a dangerous
Thrill

Contradictions

It's strange
The way
The moon
Awakens
In your eyes
When all
I see is
Sunshine
In your smile

My World and Hers

The stars
Cannot compare
To the universe
That lays
Beside me

Flowers

She was born
From glass
And raised in thorns
A lonely flower
Blooming
In the
Storm

Reminders of You

A cup of
Black coffee
With two sugars
An autumn walk
When the cold
Has not given
Way to shivers
A morning
Bed
Left unmade
The turn of a cheek
And a kiss
That refuses to fade
These
Are the simple
Reminders of you

Loose Footing

Sink
To their level
And you will loose
Your footing

Deepest Fears

I would
Wait for you forever
And I fear
That I might

What I Have Learned

Forgiveness
Is the boldest
Term for
Indifference

For You

I am meek and mild
This is true
But what I hide from
I will always give to you

Forever After

Your name
Echoes across
My tomorrows

Coffee and Sunrises

Saltines
And black coffee
She puts down her glasses
And for the first time
Sees the morning

Unrequited Journey

In my bed
She sings
The tales of her love
She will never meet

Exchange of Poison

I miss the taste of your moonlit skin
Now
I sip whiskey
From a stranger's lips
One poison for another

This Life with You

Some journeys
Are
Worth doing twice
This life
With you

Invisible Ink

She wrote her stories
In ink you couldn't see
Hoping
Someone could read between the lines

Two Songs

If the caged bird
Could sing a tune
She would sing two
One for sorrow
And one
For you

Wants and Needs

There is
A difference
Between a want
And a need
And I must learn it
When it comes
To
You

Silence

She learned
To speak
With him
Through a language
He had taught her well

Push and Pull

You belong with me
The way the moon
Dances
With the sea

Dawn to Dust

How strange
It is
For the butterflies
In my stomach
To lead me to
The graveyard
In your arms

An Endless Chance

How
Many lifetimes
Must I live
To end up
With you

Moving In

Bring
Your pain
And your suffering
In clustered boxes
And together
We will
Sort it out

Dreams

Though
Our breaths
Are finite
Our desires
Remain
Limitless

The Gender Divided

There
The laundry sat
A lack of fun
The dutiful wife
Coming undone
While
The husband
He sat
Playing mum

Employment

Darling
Love
Is a job
You must not
Quit

I Searched Galaxies

If
The sky is the limit
Then
How
Can I see
Universes
In your eyes

* 9 7 9 8 8 9 2 1 1 0 3 2 7 *